'Oh, what a commotion! What a hustle and a bustle as the tents were heaved and hauled and hoisted into position, flapping and billowing, tugging and straining at their ropes.

The big old horse gave a sigh of relief when all that confusion was over; now he could go to the five-barred gate to wait for the boy who brought him a slice of bread every morning. Only this morning the boy didn't come. This morning the boy was too excited about the Fair. He forgot the big old horse.'

And there's worse to come for the big old horse when the farmer comes along and chains him up. Why? What had he done? He was very upset...

But then disaster strikes the Fair. And it is the big old horse who comes to the rescue and makes sure all the children have a wonderful day!

THE BIG OLD HORSE

THE
BIG
OLD HORSE

EVELYN DAVIES

Illustrated by Terry Riley

YOUNG CORGI BOOKS

THE BIG OLD HORSE
A YOUNG CORGI BOOK 0 552 524719

Originally published in Great Britain by Hamish Hamilton
Children's Books

Hamish Hamilton edition published 1979
Young Corgi edition published 1988

This book is set in 14/18pt Century Textbook

Young Corgi Books are published by Transworld Publishers
Ltd., 61-63 Uxbridge Road, Ealing, London W5 5SA, in
Australia by Transworld Publishers (Australia) Pty. Ltd., 15-23
Helles Avenue, Moorebank, NSW 2170, and in New Zealand by
Transworld Publishers (N.Z.) Ltd., Cnr. Moselle and
Waipareira Avenues, Henderson, Auckland.

Made and printed in Great Britain by
The Guernsey Press Co. Ltd., Guernsey, Channel Islands.

Chapter 1

The big old horse saw the Fair
coming. Far, far away across the
fields and meadows he saw the first
caravan appear round a bend in the
road, then the second caravan and the
third and the fourth, then the wagons
and trucks and lorries trailing behind.

He opened his tired old eyes and
watched, not at all curious or con-
cerned or very interested for that

matter. Maybe he thought it was a caterpillar curving and flowing along the narrow country lanes. Maybe he thought it was a train, small and silent in the distance. Maybe he thought he was dreaming. Maybe he didn't think about it at all. Anyway

he didn't think it was anything to get excited about. At least not until it came closer, not until the caravans and wagons and trucks and lorries rumbled past his paddock and turned into the big field at the end of the lane. Then he was interested. He did get

9

excited then. He watched very curiously as wagon doors clattered open and poles and ropes and rolled up canvas tents were bundled out.

Oh, what a commotion! What a hustle and a bustle as the tents were heaved and hauled and hoisted into position, flapping and billowing, tugging and straining at their ropes. But the men, the big strong fairground men clenched their teeth and dug their heels in the ground and held on with all their might and pulled with all their strength and they soon had the poles in place, the tent pegs hammered in the ground, the ropes tightened.

The big old horse gave a sigh of relief when all that confusion was

over; now he could go to the five-
barred gate to wait for the boy who
brought him a slice of bread every
morning. Only this morning the boy
didn't come. This morning the boy
was too excited about the Fair. He
forgot the big old horse.

Chapter 2

The big old horse rested his head on the gate and waited. He dozed a little and waited very patiently. Then he dozed a little more and still waited. He went on dozing and waiting, waiting and dozing until presently he quite forgot why he was waiting. He was old and his memory was not what it was. He yawned and stretched and ambled off to crop the sweet paddock

grass. The sun warmed his back and took the stiffness out of his old bones, butterflies danced around his head and honey bees led him to the tastiest clover. He felt content and happy. He took no notice of the tents that blocked his view to the hills or the stalls and kiosks that filled the big field, but he was a little curious of all the strange noises. He pricked up his ears and leaned over the hedge to investigate and then he became very, very curious indeed.

He got quite a shock. He had seen many peculiar things in his long life, but he had never ever seen a merry-go-round before. No wonder his eyes almost popped out of his head. No wonder he got a shock ... PINK SPOTTED HORSES! Yellow and green and red and mauve horses! Horses covered in flowers and leaves and scrolls and squiggles! It just wasn't true. If he could have laughed that big old horse would have given a loud guffaw. Instead he gave a little whinny of greeting. Weird and

wonderful creatures they might be but horses they were for all that. The big old horse was quite excited. He whinnied again and leaned further over the hedge and then he got an even bigger shock.

Just at that very moment the man in charge of the merry-go-round decided to make sure everything was working properly. He flicked a switch and turned a key and pulled a lever and, yes everything was fine . . . The music blared out . . . that was bad enough but, the horses . . . Round and round they went. Round and round and up and down. Up and down, up and down on stiff brass poles. And that . . . That was too much!

The big old horse seemed about to jump clear over the hedge with fright. But he was too old and too fat. He crashed down on to it. He was half in the big field, half in his paddock. The

man in charge of the merry-go-round had quite a shock, too, when he suddenly saw him there. 'Hey,' he shouted. 'Hey! Go back! You can't come in here. Go back!' He hastily

switched off the merry-go-round and
danced about, waving his cap and his
arms in the air, very comically.

The big old horse backed away,
snorting and pawing the ground.
Tufts of grass and leaves and twigs
flew in all directions. His head went

down, his hind legs went up. He gave two or three little jumps with all four feet off the ground at the same time. Then he tore away to the farthest corner of his paddock where he stood trembling and shaking beneath an old oak tree, afraid to move, afraid to leave the sheltering branches even when the boy suddenly remembered him and came running with *two* slices of bread.

'Horse. Horse. Horse! Come quickly,' the boy called. 'Horse, I'm sorry I forgot you this morning. It was the Fair, you see. Isn't it exciting. I'm going on the swings and the wheel and the big dipper and my Dad's going to knock down a coconut.' He explained it all as he ran. But where

was the big old horse? The boy
couldn't see him beneath the oak tree.
The big old horse whinnied and shook
his head disturbing a cloud of flies.
Now the boy saw him. He came hurrying with the bread. 'Two slices to

make up for forgetting you,' he said and quickly patted the old horse's big head. He didn't stop. He was in such a hurry to go to the Fair.

Chapter 3

Presently the farmer came into the big old horse's paddock. He was trailing a length of chain behind him. It clinked and rattled. The big old horse backed away but the farmer held out a handful of sugar. The big old horse hesitated, but he just couldn't resist it. He took it daintily between his soft lips. It crunched between his teeth. The sweet taste melted in his mouth

and slipped down his throat. It was delicious. He licked and licked his lips with his long sticky tongue. He slobbered.

He didn't notice the farmer holding a big leather collar. He hardly felt it being slipped around his neck he was enjoying himself so much. He nuzzled the farmer's shoulder. The chain rattled again. And then, then he knew

what had happened. He had been
chained up! He couldn't believe it. Oh,
the disgrace. How could the farmer
have done such a thing. Why?

'Just for a while,' the farmer
explained. 'Just until I've mended
that big hole in the fence. I don't want
you getting through and hurting

yourself on any of those fairground contraptions.' But the big old horse wasn't listening. He didn't hear what the farmer was saying. He thought he had been punished. He thought he had done something wrong. He couldn't think what.

'Shan't be long,' the farmer said. He fondly rubbed the big old horse's head and hurried away to fetch some posts and nails, and a shovel to dig a hole to put the posts in and he mended that big hole in the hedge in no time at all. But when he had finished he noticed some more, smaller gaps and he thought, now what if the big old horse should get curious to see what was on the other side and push his way through. He suddenly thought, perhaps that was how the first hole had come to be there. Come to think of it, it was a rather big horse shape hole. So he decided not to take the old horse off the chain after all, not until after the Fair had moved on again.

Chapter 4

The big old horse was very upset. His head drooped, his back sagged. If he hadn't been too big and too old he would have cried. He was so sad he didn't hear thunder rumbling in the distance or notice dark clouds gathering. He was quite surprised when he felt a cold spatter of rain. The next minute lightning ripped across the

sky and a sudden burst of thunder roared and clattered directly over-head. At the same time a squally wind sprang up and rain lashed down with such force that the branches of the trees tangled together and their tall, solid trunks shivered. The grasses flattened and the hedgerows bowed before the onslaught. In the big field the caravans and wagons and trucks and lorries swayed and creaked and the wildly flapping tents seemed about to be uplifted and blown away. Again and again lightning lit up the fantastic figures of the merry-go-round horses. Water poured off their painted backs and their brass poles rattled and shook. All night the storm raged but with morning the lightning

fizzled out, the thunder died away, the clouds rolled back. The sun came out.

Now how good the air smelt. How clean and fresh the big old horse felt with all the dust washed from his coat. He lifted his head and looked about him. Water glistened in deep pools in his paddock and overflowed into the lane. The Fair people came and looked at it and went away again, shaking their heads. There would be no Fair to-day, they said. People couldn't walk through all that water. They would need boats.

'Don't worry, I'll clear the ditches,' the farmer said and he set to and dug and raked and worked very hard and by the afternoon all the water had gone. But in its place was thick black mud. The boy who lived down the lane squelched up and down in his big wellington boots. He had fun. But the

people who had come from all the nearby towns and villages to see the Fair looked up the lane in dismay. 'The children can't walk through that in their little thin shoes,' they said. 'We shall have to go home. What a wasted journey.' They were very annoyed. The children were very upset, so were the Fair people. Who ever heard of a Fair with no children to ride on the swings and the merry-go-round!

'We could carry the children in one of the trucks,' they said, 'but it would only get stuck in all that mud.'

'A tractor wouldn't be any better,' the farmer said.

The boy who lived down the lane said. 'What about the big old horse?

He could carry the children on his back. He wouldn't mind getting his feet wet.'

'A very good idea,' said the farmer. 'He could do with a bit of exercise after standing around in the rain all night.' And he went over to the big old horse and took off the leather collar from around his neck. The big old horse whinnied with delight. But then the farmer quickly put the collar back on again. 'I forgot,' he said. 'I haven't time to walk up and down the lane all the afternoon. I've the cows to milk and the pigs to feed and the hens.'

'But I could do it,' the boy said eagerly. 'I could walk up and down with the big old horse.'

'Would you?' said the farmer and he took the leather collar off the old horse's neck again. But then he looked down at the boy and he looked up at the big old horse. He shook his head. 'That won't do. You are too small,' he said. 'You could never reach up to this big old horse's forelock to lead him along.' And he put the leather collar right back on the old horse's neck and strode away, very quickly.

He was so sad the poor old horse wouldn't get his exercise after all. But then he stopped. He turned around and strode quickly back. He took off the big leather collar one more time. He put it on the ground. He picked up the boy. He sat him on the big old horse's broad back. 'There,' he said, 'you can ride the old horse up and down the lane. You are only a little

fella, after all. There is still room for
half a dozen children behind you.'

Chapter 5

Well, I don't know who was the proudest, that boy sitting high on the big old horse's back or the big old horse plodding up and down that muddy lane with all those happy, laughing, jiggety children. Right into the fairground he took them amongst the swings and the hoop-la stalls and the coconut shies. Straight to the merry-go-round that big old horse

took them. He whinnied softly to the strange painted horses and leaned forward cautiously. He didn't want to set them careering off on their stiff brass poles. But his nose nuzzled a cold, hard head and he gave a little snort of disgust. Why they weren't real horses at all. They were just . . . toys! The big old horse tossed his head and came as near as he ever would to laughing. Really he felt quite foolish.

But just then the man in charge of the merry-go-round came hurrying up waving his cap in one hand and a greasy rag in the other and shouting, 'Go back. Go back. Take all those children away again. After all we can't have the Fair today. The storm

has damaged the merry-go-round. I can't get it to work.'

Go back! Go back after the big old horse had struggled through the mud to get them there. The children's faces fell. They began to cry. 'Don't. Don't,' cried the man in charge of the merry-go-round, mopping his face with the greasy rag and leaving black streaks all over it. 'Don't cry. I'll have one more go at mending it.'

'And,' said the boy, 'this big old horse can give the children rides while you are doing it.' He clicked his tongue and the big old horse set off still chuckling to himself while the man in charge of the merry-go-round twisted some wires and mended a fuse and tightened some screws and

loosened some nuts until, at last, he got the merry-go-round to work. And by that time the big old horse was only too pleased to let the painted horses take over and go back to his paddock for a rest. But when the Fair was over all the children agreed the best part was their ride on the big old horse.

MIDNIGHT PIRATE
by Diana Hendry
Illustrated by Janet Duchesne

'Oh Pirate, dear little Pirate,' whispered Ida, 'you can't stay here. The Aunts don't want a kitten.'

Nothing Ida could say would make the Aunts change their minds and it seemed as though the tiny kitten she had found under the holly bush would have to stay out in the cold and wet, unloved by anyone.

But the kitten had other ideas and even the Aunts became involved in what happened next . . .

0 552 524174

YOUNG CORGI

A BIT OF GIVE AND TAKE
by Bernard Ashley
Illustrated by Trevor Stubley

'A kitten? You don't reckon you're keeping that, do you?' said Scott's Mum.

'I am, I saved it from death,' Scott shouted. 'He'll die without me!'

When Scott saves a kitten trapped in a rubbish bin, he takes it home despite the council rule about no pets. Scott is determined to keep Scrap, as he names the kitten, although it gets him into a lot of trouble . . .

0 552 523488

YOUNG
CORGI

A PUFF OF SMOKE
by Catherine Sefton
Illustrated by Lynne Willey

When Beaky Kelly gets up one morning feeling
bored and wishes for something to happen,
something certainly *does*. Out of his cornflakes
packet pops a Genie in a puff of blue smoke – a
Genie who has the power to grant Beaky three
wishes! The only trouble is, the Genie makes up
all the rules as he goes along and, in no time at
all, Beaky is in deep trouble at school –
especially with Mr McGrow, his bad-tempered
teacher . . .

0 552 524700

DRAGON FIRE
by Ann Ruffell
Illustrated by Andrew Brown

Gribble, the dragon, has a problem. He wakes up one morning with a sniffy nose and a throat like sandpaper. Worst of all, he can't breathe any fire to cook his breakfast!

Cadwallader, his neighbour, certainly isn't going to share any of *his* breakfast. He sends Gribble off to see the dragon doctor. But what will Gribble do if the doctor cannot help?

This is the first title in a series of adventures about Gribble, the lovable little dragon.

0 552 52445X

YOUNG CORGI

URSULA SAILING
by Sheila Lavelle
Illustrated by Thelma Lambert

Ursula is an ordinary girl – with one very special
secret. She can turn herself into a real, live, little
bear! Sometimes this can be very useful,
especially when there is a tall and difficult tree
to climb. But in this new adventure for Ursula,
she soon discovers that rivers and boats mean
trouble for bears . . .

0 552 524484

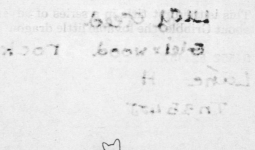

If you would like to receive a Newsletter about our new Children's books, just fill in the coupon below with your name and address (or copy it onto a separate piece of paper if you don't want to spoil your book) and send it to:

The Children's Books Editor
Young Corgi Books
61–63 Uxbridge Road,
Ealing
London W5 5SA

Please send me a Children's Newsletter:

Name .... **Lucy creed** ....

Address .. **Glirwood rock** ....

...... **Lane H** ....

...... **Tn 35 4JJ** ....

All Children's Books are available at your bookshop or newsagent, or can be ordered from the following address:
Corgi/Bantam Books,
Cash Sales Department,
P.O. Box 11, Falmouth, Cornwall TR10 9EN

Please send a cheque or postal order (no currency) and allow 60p for postage and packing for the first book plus 25p for the second book and 15p for each additional book ordered up to a maximum charge of £1.90 in UK.

B.F.P.O. customers please allow 60p for the first book, 25p for the second book plus 15p per copy for the next 7 books, thereafter 9p per book.

Overseas customers, including Eire, please allow £1.25 for postage and packing for the first book, 75p for the second book, and 28p for each subsequent title ordered.